B/S

THE JUNIOR NOVEL

D1080583

TRANSFORMERS © 2011 Hasbro. All Rights Reserved.
© 2011 Paramount Pictures Corporation. All Rights Reserved.

ISBN: 978-0-00-742867-0

1 3 5 7 9 10 8 6 4 2
First published in the UK by HarperCollins Children's Books in 2011

www.harpercollins.co.uk
Printed in Great Britain by Clays Ltd, St Ives plc

TRANS FORMERS
DARK OF THE MOON

THE JUNIOR NOVEL

Adapted by Michael Kelly
Based on the screenplay by
Ehren Kruger

HarperCollins *Children's Books*

I am Optimus Prime.

We were once a peaceful race of intelligent mechanical beings. But then came the war between the Autobots, who fought for freedom, and the Decepticons, who dreamt of tyranny.

I was there, so many millennia ago, when the battle reached a turning point. I was there when our last hope for victory and peace was lost. I remember it as though it happened cycles ago.

PROLOGUE

Many years ago, Cybertron

Optimus Prime stood on the battlefield that his home planet had become. Cybertron had once been beautiful, its gleaming towers reaching to the skies. Now it was a ruin, its cities destroyed, its lands laid to waste. The Decepticon attack had been too powerful, and little by little the Autobots had been pushed back into small pockets of resistance.

But there was a plan, and Optimus Prime watched as the great spaceship, the Ark, took off and flew overhead. For a moment, Optimus dared to think that the end of their war might be near.

Then enemy fighters took off and flew after the ship. Smaller and quicker, the Decepticons' battle cruisers closed in to attack. It would have been a quick fight if the pilot of the Autobot ship hadn't been an expert at the controls. He guided the ship through twists and turns, executing barrel rolls through ruined cities and hidden canyons. When the lone Autobot thought he had lost all pursuers, he directed the ship upward, to leave Cybertron's atmosphere and escape into space.

Optimus watched as the ship climbed higher and higher, and his hopes rose with it. But then he saw the last Decepticon fighter zoom up, and he watched as it fired its cannons. The Ark was hit. The cargo doors blew open, and the ship spun out of control.

The flaming ship spiralled into space, and Optimus Prime bowed his head. The plan had failed; the war would continue. Hope would have to be found in some other place, at some other time.

Summer 1961, the United States

The setting sun made the desert sand glow. Overhead, the moon could be seen rising into the darkening skies. In contrast to the natural landscape, rows of giant modern radio antennae swept the sky, searching for signals.

Inside, two technicians sat at the control panels. Their job was to watch the monitors for signs of anything unusual in outer space. Mostly they looked for meteors and comets – anything that might pose a danger to Earth. But what they really hoped to find was a signal from space, something that would prove there was life on other planets.

Suddenly, the computers began to beep and flash a warning: UFO DETECTED. COLLISION COURSE.

On the radar screens, they could see a dark shape drifting towards Earth. But before it could accelerate into the planet's gravitational field, the drifting object crashed onto the surface of the moon.

The scientists detected the collision on their instruments. They knew it was not a meteor. They had to tell the President that something had landed on the moon… something that might be an alien spaceship.

When he received the news, the President called the director of NASA and said, "I want men on the moon in this decade. We need to know what crashed up there, and we need to know before anyone else."

The director of NASA stood in the Mission Control room. He listened to the radio message on the speakers. A crackly voice said, "The Eagle has landed."

Without warning, the transmission from the moon went dead. Everyone in Mission Control began to scramble, checking monitors, typing codes.

"What happened?" demanded the director.

"Seems to be a transmitter malfunction," replied a technician.

"Well, get it back up! Get our men back in contact!" the director growled.

Communication was not down, though. Unknown to the director, a secret second control room had been set up near Mission Control. In that room, hidden from everyone, stood three men in black suits. One of them spoke into a microphone.

"Eagle, you are dark on the rock. Mission is a go. You have twenty one minutes."

On the moon, astronauts Buzz Aldrin and Neil Armstrong were trying to get used to walking in low gravity. They did not have much time, and they bounced along the moon's surface in their bulky space suits. Behind them, their ship, the Eagle, stood waiting, an American flag planted beside it.

The astronauts climbed a hill and stood in shocked amazement. In front of them, a huge spaceship lay wrecked on the ground. The astronauts found a hole in the side of the ship and climbed inside.

The strange craft had been badly damaged when it crashed. Moon dust covered everything, and the astronauts had to pick their way carefully over the rubble. Several times they nearly fell into gaping holes, but they managed to get through and finally stood in what was probably the control room of the giant ship.

The astronauts could see the shape of a gigantic metal robot lying in the dust.

"Houston, we've got extraterrestrials. No sign of movement or life," Armstrong reported.

"Roger, we copy. Take photos and samples and get home," came the response. "I guess we are not alone after all."

"No, sir," replied Aldrin. "We are not alone."

CHAPTER I

Present day, Washington, D.C.

Sam Witwicky was asleep. At least, he wanted to be asleep. Sam did not have a job, and getting out of bed meant another day of interviews and looking for work.

Sam's new girlfriend, Carly, called out, "My hero needs to wake up! Today is the day!" She came into Sam's room holding a giant stuffed white bunny. Sam peeked at her over his covers, saw the rabbit, and then pulled the covers back over his head.

"What is that?" he groaned.

"It's a rabbit! For luck!" said Carly.

Sam sat up. He reached out and grabbed the rabbit's foot. "Um, Carly, love the thought, but it's supposed to be just a rabbit's foot, not the whole thing!"

"Well, you need more luck than just a foot," Carly laughed. "Anyway, it's to get you thinking positively. Wear your nice tie."

"Do you know how demoralising it is to have saved the world – twice – and to still be begging for a job?" Sam asked as she left the room.

"People don't know you saved the world, Sam," she said over her shoulder. "I mean, I do. I believe you."

Sam froze. "Whoa, what does that mean? It sounds like you don't believe me."

"I wasn't there, Sam. Bad choice of words."

"I should be working with the Autobots," Sam said with a sigh.

"Well, at least they paid for your college," said Carly. "And the President gave you the hero medal."

Sam thought back to when he met the President. He had been given a medal for helping Optimus Prime, Bumblebee and the other Autobots stop The Fallen and the rest of the Decepticons from destroying the world. He'd enjoyed meeting the President, but he also met Carly that day. He enjoyed meeting her even more.

Carly called him back from his memories. "Hey, time to move on!" she said. "Getting a job is hard for everyone. But I know you can do it!"

There was a knock on the balcony door. Outside, Sam could see Wheelie, the small blue remote-control truck turned robot he had met during his last adventure with the Autobots. Wheelie now lived with Sam, along with another small Transformer named Brains. They both wanted to come into the apartment.

"Ugh, they give me the creeps," said Carly. "I'm going to be late for work, and I just started this job. I have to go."

Sam watched Carly leave, then turned back to the two robots outside. Sam shrugged and walked over to the sliding door to let in Wheelie and Brains.

"It's not fair," cried Wheelie. "She makes us live in the garden!"

"You and your sidekick cannot be in here without permission," said Sam. "I'm serious. You know how long it took me to get over Mikaela. I don't want to lose Carly because of you two."

Sam looked over at Brains, who was sitting on the floor eating metal screws out of a dog dish. Sam just shook his head.

"Okay, stop with the screws. Look, you guys like it here, right? Just treat Carly with respect."

Sam looked at the clock and said, "Uh-oh!" He was going to be late! He ran for the shower.

CHAPTER 2

Pripyat, Ukraine

A light snow was falling from the grey sky. The landscape was devoid of sound: No birds sang, no children played. All was still.

The silence was suddenly broken by the roar of a NEST convoy speeding down the deserted road. In the lead, a big-rig eighteen-wheel semi-truck roared along the road. The truck was covered in ice and mud, but glinting through were patches of red and blue. Behind the truck drove an emergency rescue vehicle, which in turn was followed by several military Humvees.

NEST stood for Non-biological Extraterrestrial Species Treaty and had come about thanks to the Autobots – Transformers who came from Cybertron to live peacefully on Earth, in harmony with the humans. The NEST soldiers and other personnel worked hand in hand with Optimus Prime and his fellow Autobots to fight the Decepticon threat and keep Earth safe.

As they rounded a bend in the road, the city of Pripyat came into view. It was a ghost town. On the edge of the city, an amusement park stood silently. A towering Ferris wheel rusted against the skyline, and bumper cars peeked from behind years of overgrown vines. The city showed signs of a rapid evacuation, with household items – even toys – scattered about everywhere. In the distance, faint music could be heard.

The convoy stopped at a set of huge gates. Colonel Lennox climbed down from the cab of the truck and looked around at the scene of desolation. He was wearing a full-body radiation suit.

Lennox explained to his companions, "This is where the Chernobyl power plant workers lived until the accident in 1986. It's not expected to be inhabitable again for hundreds, maybe thousands, of years. They play that music so the clean up crews don't go insane from the loneliness. But it just makes everything spookier."

A man in his late fifties named Voskhod stood beside Lennox. He had secretly reached out to Lennox and his team with some information: there was something here they needed to see – something alien.

"Come," said Voskhod. "Our destination is a bit further up the road." He unlocked the heavy gate and climbed back into his car.

The convoy continued along the road, skirting the edge of Pripyat. Ahead of them loomed the Chernobyl nuclear reactor. The reactor had melted down in 1986, releasing deadly radiation into the air, soil and water. The entire area had to be evacuated.

Since then, the reactor building had been encased in a gigantic concrete sarcophagus. The convoy came to a halt in front of the massive structure.

Lennox and Voskhod exited their vehicles, while numerous scientists and soldiers deployed from the convoy of Humvees. Then, with a mechanical rumbling, the semi and the emergency vehicle converted into towering robots. Optimus Prime and Ratchet surveyed the scene.

The two Autobots were too large to enter the reactor building itself, so Optimus and Ratchet waited outside while Lennox and his men followed Voskhod.

As they descended into the lower levels, Lennox saw the effects of the meltdown of the nuclear core. The fuel rods had become like lava, flowing through steel and concrete at unimaginable temperatures. The after-effects of these lava flows were more and more visible as the men went deeper into the facility.

Voskhod explained what they were seeing as they walked. "There were energy experiments going on in this reactor. Every year, our clean up efforts probe deeper. Only days ago we found it."

The group continued into the core, passing rooms that were filled with debris and old office equipment. Finally, they stood outside a room that had been mostly filled with the radioactive lava. An area had recently been cleared of debris, and

Lennox looked at the object that had been revealed.

Lennox had been working for the Autobots for six years now, and he had seen some crazy stuff. So he knew immediately that he was looking at something from Cybertron. He radioed to Optimus Prime.

"Optimus, we have a visual. Object is in some sort of metal harness. There's also a case." He then looked to the scientists, asking, "Guys, are these markings from the Soviet space programme?"

He never got an answer. At that moment, the room began to tremble and shake.

CHAPTER 3

Chernobyl nuclear facility, Pripyat, Ukraine

A technician looked up from his scanner and shouted, "Energon reading. Sir, it's strong… below us… closing fast!"

Lennox sprang into action. He knew that whatever it was, it probably wasn't friendly. "Everybody abort. Move topside. Now!"

The room exploded in chaos. Dirt and stone shot up from the floor in a huge blast, and Lennox looked on in horror as huge metallic tentacles whirled up from the hole. The tentacles reached for two of the scientists.

Lennox quickly shouted orders: "Take cover! Decepticon! Optimus, we have unknown enemy contact. Moving back to the surface!"

The team ran back through the maze of stairs

and hallways as the floor behind them writhed with the snakelike metal feelers. Lennox paused to look back as his men ran by, and watched as one of the clawed tentacles grabbed the mysterious object.

As they finally ran outside, Lennox yelled, "Defensive positions! Anything comes out of that building, light it up!" He had barely finished speaking when an entire section of the reactor's wall blew out towards them. Through the dust and flying rubble, they could see the whirling tentacles of the monstrous creature. It still clutched the artifact in its claw.

Optimus Prime recognised the creature immediately, but he couldn't understand why he was seeing it at this time and place. It was a Cybertronian Driller, and Optimus had not laid eyes on one since leaving Cybertron. He had also never seen one grown to such an enormous size.

Back on Cybertron, Drillers were used for mining operations. They were beasts more than anything. The Transformers raised them and trained them to bore into Cybertron, making tunnels, excavating resources. But typically they grew to no more than fifteen or twenty feet.

Optimus Prime estimated that the Driller in front of him had to be more than one hundred feet long, and he could see only part of it. He could also see that it had been enhanced. This one looked less suited to mining, and more ready for military action.

Suddenly, the Driller stopped moving. With a hissing sound, a section at the top slid back, revealing a cockpit. The driver stepped out and scanned his surroundings. His single, glowing eye swept over the NEST soldiers and came to rest on the Autobot leader.

"Shockwave!" Optimus exclaimed in surprise.

Shockwave had been one of Megatron's most trusted soldiers and advisors back on Cybertron. He approached every situation with the mind of a pure scientist: calculating, detached, emotionless. It was these qualities that made him one of the most feared of all Decepticons. Optimus thought Shockwave had stayed behind on Cybertron, but there was no mistaking it: the single eye, the arm ending in a fusion cannon, the air of menace. Shockwave had come to Earth.

Optimus transmitted a silent command to his truck trailer, and it suddenly shifted form into a mobile battle station.

As Shockwave levelled his blaster arm at the NEST soldiers, Optimus pulled a huge shield from the battle station. He barked a command: "Lennox, you and your men, get behind me. NOW!"

Shockwave unleashed a blast of plasma. Optimus leaned into the blast, deflecting the heat and pressure away from the men. Extending his own cannon, Optimus began to return fire in a rapid stream at both Shockwave and the Driller.

The Decepticon sensed that the time was not right. His mission was to retrieve the artefact, not engage the Autobot leader. That time would come. For now, he returned to his cockpit and coaxed the Driller back into the hole from which it had emerged.

Optimus sensed the danger of letting Shockwave escape with the prize and leapt after the Driller, his sword extended. With a single sweep, he severed the tentacle that was clutching the artefact. The Driller disappeared in a rumbling frenzy.

Walking over to get a closer look, Optimus could see that the artefact was cylindrical in shape, and shone with the glint of dull steel. "It can't be," he whispered.

Lennox ordered his men back to their vehicles and then turned to Optimus Prime. "What was that thing? And why was it after this?"

But Optimus barely heard Lennox's questions. He muttered to himself, "It's simply impossible." Then, remembering Lennox, he turned to him and said, "This is an engine part... from a long-lost Autobot ship."

CHAPTER 4

Downtown Washington, D.C.

Sam blinked his eyes as he walked into the bright sunlight. A day full of interviews would give anyone a headache. The only thing he wanted to do now was get back to his apartment, get out of his suit, and wait for Carly to come over. Maybe they could have a quiet dinner together, with no interviews, and no robots.

His mobile phone chimed. He looked at it and saw a text from Carly. Sam smiled, happy to hear from her. But then he frowned as he read the text.

LATE ADD. FINAL INTERVIEW OF THE DAY: ACCURETTA SYSTEMS.

Sam sighed and put his phone back into his pocket. He wondered if this day would ever end.

Sam sat in the office of Bruce Brazos, Senior Vice President of Personnel. Sam slumped in his chair. He really did not want to be sitting through another interview. Bruce, on the other hand, seemed to be relishing the moment. He reminded Sam a little too much of the guy who had sold him the old banger he had been driving since Bumblebee left for a special mission.

"Okay," began Bruce, "I got myself a 'Sam Witwicky', recent college graduate, previous experience next to zero, but hmm... he's got a recommendation letter from one of our board members!"

That surprised Sam. "That's nice, but... do I know someone on your board?"

"Here's the deal," Bruce continued, ignoring Sam's question. "You know who we are. Accuretta Systems, global leader in telecom and aerospace, seventeen billion dollars in profit last year. We contract for DARPA, NASA, you name it. You perform here, doors open for you anywhere. Kids who sat in your chair run Congress now, and own major corporations. You know what they have in common? Me.

"First job outta college is critical, kid. Now, are you a go-getter? A take-charge kind of guy? We're not looking for that here. I want a machine. Follows my orders, questions nothing."

Sam raised his eyebrows. This sounded weird.

"You start in the mailroom," Bruce continued. "You know who else started there? Me. And the CEO. So I'm giving you ninety seconds here: impress me."

Sam sighed. He didn't want to work in a mailroom. "You know, I'm really looking for the right job. I just… Thanks, but I don't think it's going to work out." Sam stood up and turned to the door to leave.

Bruce was taken completely off guard. No one walked out of Bruce Brazos's office mid-interview. No one.

"What the… You don't think? You?"

Sam turned back and looked at Bruce. "Mister, I saved your life – twice. I can't tell you when, where, or how, but rest assured, I have done stuff that matters. And I want a job where I matter again. Thank you." Sam turned again and walked to the door – only to find himself standing face-to-face with Bruce.

"What's your story, Witwicky? Walking out on my interview? No one's ever done that before. You really don't want this job, do you? You want the job after it. And the one after that. But this job's the one in your way. And that's why you're going to be good at it. That's right, no secrets here. Because I look at you and see a younger me!"

Bruce poked Sam in the chest, backing him up until Sam fell into the chair.

"Nine AM tomorrow," Bruce insisted. "I'd say I just found my new company man."

Sam wasn't quite sure what had just happened, but he had a job! He might as well keep it until he found a better one. He got into his car and drove to see Carly at her new office.

When Sam pulled up in front of the building, he

had to double-check the address. He drove his car along a winding drive that ended at the waterfront. Over the wharf rose a towering structure of glass and steel. This was where Carly worked?

Entering the foyer, Sam felt as though he were in a museum. In a daze, he wandered up to the front desk.

"Um… Carly Spencer? She just started here?" Sam asked, feeling awkward.

The receptionist pointed him down a vast hall, and Sam noticed Carly standing next to two exotic cars, talking on her mobile phone. Carly saw Sam and ended her call.

"Sam! You really got a job? See? What'd I tell you? The bunny worked!"

Sam felt uncomfortable. He looked at the cars; he looked up at the glass ceiling. He felt really out of place in the expensive surroundings. At that moment, Carly's boss walked up and introduced himself: "I'm Dylan Gould. It's a pleasure to meet you. Carly told me all about you."

"Thanks. Nice, uh, place you have here."

"Come with me – you've got to see my garage," Dylan said, leading them through a large door to a huge warehouse space.

Some people collect stamps, some people collect action figures. Dylan Gould collected cars. His garage consisted of row upon row of classic cars, exotic cars, and classic exotic cars. If it was worth lots and lots of money, Dylan had it in his collection.

"My dad built an empire," Dylan explained. "We're one of the largest accounting firms in the United States. I started up the venture side after he passed. It's a gambler's game, really, Sam. I collect cars just to keep my sanity."

Sam looked away from the vehicle Dylan was droning on about and began to study the photos on the wall. This was Dylan's wall of fame. Sam recognised practically everyone in the pictures: politicians, actresses, business leaders, and more actresses.

"You an aficionado, Sam?" Dylan asked him. "What do you drive?"

"Sam used to drive this amazing Camaro," Carly offered.

"One of a kind. Lots of special features," added Sam.

"Outstanding ride. Like your taste." Dylan looked at Carly. "I mean, it's quite evident."

That was enough for Sam: He didn't like this guy. "So, I just came by to take Carly home," he said, and then he led her outside to the embarrassingly shabby car, trailed by Dylan. Sam got in and turned the key. The engine made a sound like a honking swan.

Sam got out, popped the bonnet, and started prodding wires. He tried to ignore Dylan, who had come up to look over his shoulder with bemused horror.

"It's a rare model car. Very… vintage," Sam muttered.

"Looks like a train wreck," countered Dylan. "Sam, Carly told me you've been looking for a job. Just so you know, I'm on the board at Accuretta Systems. So I put in a call. Hope it helped."

Thankfully, at that moment the car came back to life. Dylan gave Sam a friendly pat on the back and then waved as he and Carly drove away.

Sam forced a smile as Carly kissed him on the cheek. It had been a very weird day. He wasn't sure about his girlfriend's new boss. And he really wasn't sure about the new job that her new boss had helped him get.

CHAPTER 5

NEST headquarters, secret location outside Washington, D.C.

Optimus Prime was angry. When the humans and Autobots had formed an alliance, part of the agreement had been complete honesty between the two species. The Autobots told the humans everything they needed to know about the history of the Transformers, and the humans promised to tell the Autobots everything they knew about past contact with alien life.

The Autobots had lived up to their end of the bargain; the humans had not. Optimus knew he had been lied to, and he was furious.

Optimus was in his truck mode, parked in the main hangar at NEST headquarters. He hadn't spoken to anyone in hours, and his fellow Autobots were getting nervous. They knew he had been brooding over the Cybertronian fuel cell, which now stood before him on a pedestal.

Lennox came into the hangar, walking swiftly to keep up with the woman marching at his side. She led them right up to Optimus.

Lennox made introductions. "Optimus, you remember Charlotte Mearing, our Director of National Intelligence?" If trucks could glower, Optimus Prime was doing so at that moment.

Director Mearing was unimpressed. "What's this, the alien silent treatment?"

Suddenly, in a scramble of moving parts, Optimus changed from truck form to robot. He lowered his head to Mearing's height and got right in her face. "You lied to us!" he shouted. Optimus kicked the pedestal, and the fuel cell clattered to the floor at Mearing's feet.

"Is that for effect?" she asked. Mearing was annoyed. She was a person others feared. Senators, generals, special agents – they all deferred to her. She had no intention of bowing down to an alien robot. Especially an alien robot throwing a tantrum.

"Everything humans know of our planet was supposedly shared with us," Optimus continued. "So why was this found in human possession?"

"Optimus, I assure you," said Mearing, "At the CIA, the FBI, we were in the dark on this. It was director-only clearance at Sector Seven. Until now. This was a secret few men knew. And fewer still remain alive."

As she spoke, a small group of men approached. One, despite having left youth far behind him, was clearly a leader of men. He looked at Optimus with an expression that conveyed both reverence and camaraderie.

"Meet two of NASA's founding mission directors, and astronaut Buzz Aldrin – one of the first two men to set foot on the moon." Mearing stepped aside to make room, and Aldrin walked straight up to Optimus.

"From a fellow space explorer to another: it's an honour," Aldrin said.

"The honour is mine," replied Optimus.

Mearing explained, "Our entire space race of the 1960s, it appears, was in response to an event."

"We were sworn to secrecy by our commander in chief," continued Aldrin. "Our mission was for mankind and science, yes. But there was also a military component: to investigate a crashed alien ship. Its cargo hold was empty. No survivors aboard."

"The Soviets managed to land unmanned probes. They must have somehow picked up that fuel cell," added the mission director.

Mearing turned to a television monitor and pushed the PLAY button. On the monitor, a grainy black-and-white image appeared. The image showed Soviet scientists working in a lab. The fuel cell was on the table in front of them.

"This is a security video obtained in 1986. We believe the Russians deduced it was a fissionable fuel assembly, and tried to harness it at Chernobyl."

As the group watched, the scientists on the video threw a switch, and immediately the scene switched to one of utter chaos. Instrument panels showed gauges pegged in the red zone, and a high-pitched whine emitted from the TV. Suddenly, the screen flashed with brilliant white light, and then went dark.

"Obviously, not the best use of judgment," Mearing observed. "Russian intelligence, of course, maintains that this incident never occurred."

"We landed six missions in total, obtained thousands of photos and samples," said Aldrin.

"But you searched it entirely?" asked Optimus. "Including its crash vault?"

The scientists looked at each other uncertainly, clearly thinking, crash vault?

Buzz replied, "We only had enough oxygen for three hours on the surface. Barely twenty minutes in the ship."

Optimus thought for some time. The implications of this information were almost overwhelming. But he resolved to continue trusting his human allies.

"The ship was named the Ark," he explained. "I watched it escape Cybertron myself. It was carrying an Autobot technology that could have won us the war. And its captain, the great Sentinel Prime, was the technology's inventor. He was commander of the Autobots before me."

"Then the Decepticons are hunting for that ship," said Lennox.

"It's imperative that I find it before the Decepticons learn of its location," Optimus replied gravely. "You must launch another moon mission. And you must pray it is in time."

CHAPTER 6

An arid savanna in Namibia

The sun beat down on the road. In the distance, a dust cloud rose. A bevy of swans was disturbed by the noise and took off in flight, rising over the savanna.

An old Russian oil tanker rumbled along the plains. It was stopped by a herd of water buffalo, wallowing in the roadway. And then it became a mass of twisting metal, rising into the dreadful shape of Megatron.

The once proud leader of the Decepticons, hunchbacked and leaking Energon from his devastated face, slouched across the road and made for a sheltered clearing. In the clearing Megatron sat heavily upon the ground to rest. With a roar and a cloud of dust, Starscream arrived and landed right in front of Megatron.

"My brave and wise master! Starscream heeds your call! It pains me to see you so wounded, so helpless, so weak…"

Even damaged and weakened, Megatron was still more than a match for his upstart lieutenant. He looked up at Starscream with a warning in his eyes.

"No harm meant, my lord!" grovelled Starscream. "It's an excellent strategy: hiding! Hiding and scheming. It's going very well!"

"Silence, you insipid fool!" roared Megatron. "You know what you are told, which is nothing. While I lay prisoner here those many years, beneath their wretched dam, Soundwave was watching over this planet. Perhaps you remember a ship called the Ark…"

Seemingly from out of nowhere, as if on cue, Soundwave entered the camp. He was Megatron's master spy. A smaller, birdlike Decepticon named Laserbeak landed on his shoulder with a sadistic purr.

"It has been found, Lord Megatron. By the

Autobots," reported Soundwave.

"Then let the Autobots do our work for us. Let them bring the ship's cargo to me." Megatron gazed up at the full moon, rising into the African sky. "And as for your 'human' collaborators, Soundwave, it is time to ensure their silence."

CHAPTER 7

The surface of the moon

Optimus Prime and Ratchet walked across the lunar surface from the NASA craft to the Ark. To maintain secrecy, the Autobots' mission had been disguised as a routine satellite launch from an Air Force base.

Much like their predecessors Neil Armstrong and Buzz Aldrin, Optimus and Ratchet found themselves looking over the wreck of the Ark. Optimus nodded at Ratchet, and the two proceeded to venture inside. Where the Earth astronauts were frightened and awed by what they found there, the two Transformers felt different emotions: sadness and loss.

They approached the crash vault as if they were entering a sacred tomb. Optimus activated a keypad, which revealed seven glowing glyphs. As though he had just entered it yesterday, Optimus punched in the code, and the vault swung open. Inside lay Sentinel Prime. Optimus and Ratchet bowed their heads.

Surrounding Sentinel Prime were five metallic pillars with Cybertronian symbols all over them. Optimus looked at Ratchet and nodded. Ratchet picked up the pillars and headed back to their NASA ship. Optimus carried the body of Sentinel to the lunar lander and prepared for the return trip to Earth.

Unseen by either Autobot, however, were several creeping things that flitted from shadow to shadow on the lunar surface. As the craft lifted off, the things revealed themselves and scampered towards the ship. Leaping, they caught hold of the belly of the ship, and then slid into hiding.

Optimus was returning to Earth with the body of his old leader. He was also returning with three stowaways, and their intentions were not friendly.

CHAPTER 8

Accuretta Systems office, Washington, D.C.

Sam walked through the aisles of cubicles, delivering mail. Once in a while, a co-worker would call his name or thank him for a letter. But Sam acknowledged them only with a nod of his head or a casual wave. His mind was on other things. Like how he was handing out mail in an office instead of helping to keep the world safe.

Unbeknownst to Sam, a man was watching his every move as Sam walked down the hallway and pressed the button for the lift. Sam hummed while he waited, and didn't notice the figure peering around the corner at him. The lift doors opened, and Sam pushed the trolley in between the other riders. Just as the doors started to close, a running figure jumped into the lift.

When the doors opened everyone exited the lift, and Sam tried to do the same, but he found his path blocked.

"Mailroom boy, you can't hide from me! Don't respond to my e-mails?"

"Uh, I'm sorry, do you work here?" Sam asked, startled.

"Shh! No names! Not Safe! Not here! I know you! I know who you are!"

Sam wanted to get away from this guy. When the lift door opened again, he pushed past the man and walked quickly down the hall. Unfortunately, the strange man followed.

"No, you're him. Little guy from the news. FBI manhunt, whole world was looking for you. I got you with aliens. You showed up on the background of six different photos, two continents, with aliens. That was you, in Egypt! Because you know aliens!"

Sam abandoned the mail trolley and started to run away from his pursuer. Before he knew it, he was being shoved into an empty office. The guy locked the door and turned to him.

"I'm Jerry Wang."

"Uh… Sir, do I know you?" asked Sam.

Jerry was fidgeting and waving his hands. "They watch, they listen – everywhere – can't go to the government, but you – you can! Why you think no one's been up there since 1972?"

"Sir," tried Sam, "I know you are speaking English, but it's not normal English…"

Without warning, Jerry pulled up his trouser leg and revealed a large yellow envelope taped to his calf. He pulled it off and forced it into Sam's unwilling hands.

Jerry went on in a tone that landed somewhere between a shout and a whisper. "My manifesto! They want us all silenced. Everyone who knows… what's on the dark side! Your alien friends are in danger! You know the good ones. It's up to you."

With that, Jerry unlocked the door and burst out of the office.

Sam sat at his desk and leafed through Jerry's manifesto, which had been in the envelope. However

OPTIMUS PRIME

BUMBLEBEE

SENTINEL PRIME

MEGATRON

SHOCKWAVE

SKIDS

MUDFLAP

IRONHIDE

weird Jerry was, it was clear that the information he had compiled was real, and frightening. Sam left his office and took the lift up to the Aerospace Division.

Sam tentatively approached Jerry's office. The door was open a crack, and Sam read the nameplate: JERRY WANG, VP, SATELLITE RESEARCH AND DEVELOPMENT. Sam heard Jerry having an animated conversation, but it seemed to Sam that he was talking to himself.

"But I did it! I did what you want!" said Jerry.

Sam pushed the door open and looked into the office. The moment Jerry noticed him, he stopped talking and moved as if to block something from Sam's view.

"You!" shouted Jerry angrily. "Why you bothering me? Can't you see I'm working, total stranger lost office boy?"

Now Sam was completely confused. "But – I'm Sam…"

"One phone call, I'll have you fired! Knock first!"

Sam blinked. *What is with this guy?* he

wondered. Sam looked around the room suspiciously, but the only odd thing he noticed was that Jerry had two computers on his desk. They were identical in design, except that one was white, and one was black.

"Is something… wrong?" Sam asked.

"Never met you. Leave me be!" shouted Jerry.

As Sam backed out of the office, he noticed Jerry's hand on the mouse of the black computer. Then he noticed that the mouse had teeth.

"Uh… I'll come back… Wrong office…" Sam mumbled.

Had he remained, Sam would have seen the black computer change into Laserbeak, and Jerry's one-sided conversation would have made sense.

"Don't know him! I'd never say anything!" Jerry pleaded with the Decepticon. "What more do you want from me?"

"Mission abort, moon man," Laserbeak hissed. "Decepticons no need you any more."

Sam hurried away from Jerry's office and took

the stairs back down to his floor. He had one thought in his mind: *I've gotta get out of here.* But just as he was deciding between the stairs and the lift, the cubicle next to him exploded.

It was Laserbeak, and he was after Sam!

"What did the moon man have to say?"

Sam turned and took a running dive onto the mail trolley, which rolled down the hallway with Laserbeak in pursuit. Sam crashed into the wall and fell off, but he was up again in an instant and dove into the computer room. Sam crept between the machines, making his way towards the door on the opposite wall.

Laserbeak caught sight of him as he made a dash for the door, and Sam scrambled out as servers exploded behind him in a hail of fire. Sam, panting, locked the door behind him. He didn't stop running until he got to his car. For once, the old Datsun worked just fine.

Sam stopped at home to grab Carly, Wheelie and Brains, and then peeled out. The Datsun screeched to a halt in front of a gated building. The sign on the fence read HEALTH & HUMAN SERVICES, but Sam knew it was the secret base of NEST. Two heavily armed guards approached him.

"Open the gate!" cried Sam. "We've gotta talk to Colonel Lennox! We're reporting a Decepticon. The Decepticons are back!"

"Sam, where are we?" asked Carly.

"Sir, this is Health and Human Services," said the guard.

"Don't give me that," Sam argued. "Let me talk to Optimus."

"Sir," replied the guard firmly, "You've made some mistake. Step out of the vehicle."

"Sam, are you sure you're at the right place?" Carly asked.

"I'm Sam Witwicky – don't you know who I am? What part of 'Decepticons are back' do you not understand?" Sam could see he wasn't getting anywhere. He nodded to the guard, and then slammed his foot down on the accelerator. He did not get far. The car managed to break through the gate, but immediately two steel barriers shot up from the ground. Sam's Datsun was sandwiched between them. At the same time, alarms began to blare.

"We've got an Energon reading!" shouted the guard. "Get out of the car!"

Guards came running from every direction. While one guard struggled with Sam, another peered into the backseat of the crushed Datsun, where he saw Wheelie and Brains staring back at him, frightened.

"Got aliens inside the vehicle!" he shouted. "Freeze!"

"Just tell Bumblebee!" Sam pleaded. "Is Bee in there?"

Sam was pushed roughly to the ground. With his face on the concrete, Sam began to yell into the walkie-talkie the guard had strapped to his leg. "Can anyone hear me? This is Sam Witwicky!"

Finally, a bright yellow Camaro came speeding out of the NEST hangar, changing into a massive robot as it approached the gates. As gently as he could, Bumblebee pushed the guards off of Sam and helped his friend stand up.

No matter how many times she saw it, Carly just couldn't get used to it. "Hello, Bumblebee," she gasped. "Long time no see."

Sam dusted himself off and walked a short distance away. Bumblebee followed.

"What's with you, huh?" Sam asked. "I know your secret-mission stuff is important, but we never see you any more. You can't even spend one night in the garage, just to hang?"

Bumblebee hung his head, pouting. His voice had been damaged in battle, and while he managed to get his point across through songs and clips he borrowed from the radio, he simply couldn't find the right words for this moment.

"Yeah, I hope you feel bad," Sam continued. "You should feel bad." He paused for a moment. Then he couldn't help smiling at his friend. "Look at this thing I'm driving now!" he said, pointing to the Datsun. "I feel bad every day!" he joked.

Bumblebee put his hands up, as if to say, *What do you want me to do about it?* and the two friends walked inside together.

CHAPTER 9

NEST headquarters, secret location outside Washington, D.C.

Sam and Carly hurried across the lobby of NEST headquarters, trailed by several guards. Sam was relieved to see a familiar face. Colonel Lennox was just coming out of a briefing room, and he called to them with surprise. "Sam, Carly, what are you doing here?"

Sam wanted to say, I should be working here every day, but instead he went with, "OK, everybody raise your hand if a flying psycho-ninja computer tried to kill you today. No? Just me?"

Sam handed Lennox the envelope containing Jerry Wang's manifesto. Lennox had just begun to look through the materials in the envelope when Director Mearing walked up.

"Excuse me. What's going on?" Mearing asked.

As Lennox flipped through the documents, his expression changed from surprise to alarm. Sam ignored the presence of Director Mearing and continued speaking directly to Lennox. "He recognised me... said I need to warn you... something about the dark side of the moon."

"He mentioned the moon?" asked Lennox.

"But why would Decepticons want to hurt humans?" asked Carly. "I thought their war was with the Autobots."

"I'd say they're after what we just found," replied Lennox.

"Excuse me, Colonel Lennox!" Director Mearing was furious. She did not know exactly what was going on, but she knew he shouldn't be telling government secrets to a couple of kids.

"Director Mearing," explained Lennox, "this is Sam Witwicky. He's the civilian who—"

"I know his name, Colonel. I want to know who gave him clearance."

"How about Optimus Prime, when he landed in

front of my house?" offered Sam.

"Disrespect of a federal official," Mearing snapped. "And who's this?"

"Carly, my girlfriend."

"Carly knows all about the Autobots, Director," said Lennox. "I can vouch for her."

"Well, thank you, Colonel," Mearing replied. "Now let's find someone to vouch for you."

"How about we talk about the Decepticon that tried to murder me today?" asked Sam impatiently.

"Um, Sam, this is the U.S. Intelligence Director," warned Lennox. "She can authorise bad things to happen for the rest of your life."

"Well, that sounds illegal," scoffed Sam.

Mearing flashed Sam a sinister smile, and he backed down under her withering gaze. Lennox broke the tension by handing Mearing Jerry Wang's manifesto.

"A software engineer at Sam's office was involved with NASA's moon-mapping probe…"

Klaxon horns blared throughout the facility, breaking up the conversation. Something big was about to happen. Director Mearing turned on her heels and stalked off towards the observation platform that had been assembled in the main hangar, with Lennox walking beside her. Sam and Carly found themselves flanked by two NEST soldiers, and followed.

Sam looked down from the observation platform. Below him, steel girders had been assembled in a shape that looked like an enormous throne. Supported by this structure was the massive bulk of Sentinel Prime. No sign of life came from the silent form.

On the far side of the room, NEST personnel were loading the five mysterious pillars into a secure vault.

The voice of Colonel Lennox barked over a loudspeaker: "Optimus, you are authorised to attempt contact."

Optimus Prime stood before his old commander and pulled open his chest plate. An intense beam of light fell upon the sleeping colossus.

Lennox whispered to Mearing, "That's the

Matrix of Leadership. One of the only things in the universe that can re-power a Transformer." Mearing only nodded in reply, transfixed by the events below.

"Sentinel Prime… we bid you return," said Optimus as he plunged the Matrix of Leadership into the chest of Sentinel Prime. The results were instantaneous. A pulse of pure energy surged through Sentinel and his back arched. With all the skill of the ultimate warrior, Sentinel leapt up from his makeshift throne, then grabbed Optimus and threw him to the ground. In the same movement, his forearm extended in a deadly blade, pointed directly at Optimus's Spark.

All around the room, NEST soldiers brought their weapons to firing position, terrified yet unsure of how to proceed.

"Hold your fire! Hold your fire!" Lennox shouted in urgent command.

"Sentinel… it is I," said Optimus calmly.

Sentinel Prime looked into the face before him and recognised Optimus Prime. Lowering his sword arm, he looked around the room, noticing the other

Autobots, as well as their human companions. In a flash his memories returned, and he thought back to the Ark, spinning out of control, drifting into space. He remembered locking himself within the crash vault, and the uncertainty he had felt at the time as to whether he would ever look upon a living Transformer again.

"We are here. You are safe," Optimus reassured him.

At that moment, Optimus, Ironhide and the other Autobots each fell to one knee, in reverence to their fallen leader, returned to them beyond hope.

"The war?" asked Sentinel.

"The war was lost," replied Optimus.

"And Cybertron... our home?" continued Sentinel.

"It was left a barren wasteland, under Decepticon control. It is dying. Like its whole galaxy. A small band of us have taken refuge here on planet Earth. We have formed an alliance with its human race."

Sentinel looked around the room, and then back to Optimus Prime. "Stand, young Optimus," he said kindly. Optimus stood eye-to-eye with his old mentor.

"You are, and always have been, the bravest warrior I have ever known," Sentinel told him. "In my escape, the ship was damaged…"

"You saved five pillars, Sentinel."

"Only five," mused Sentinel. "Once we had hundreds."

Director Mearing walked out onto the gantry, unperturbed by the drama of the recent events, and edged past Lennox to address the two leaders.

"Autobots. What is this technology you were trying to save?"

"Together," explained Sentinel, "The pillars form a Space Bridge. I designed it, and I alone can control it. It defies the laws of physics to transport matter through time and space. It was to be our key to winning the war."

"You're talking about a teleportation device," said Mearing.

"For resources. Refugees…" said Optimus.

"Or soldiers. Weapons. Bombs. A means of

instant strike," countered Mearing. "That's the military function, isn't it?"

Sentinel's reply was firm, but not angry. "If my ship had escaped, we could have transported all Autobots to a safe haven. It is our technology. And it must be returned."

"Yes. When the human race says so," said Mearing. "You don't just bring weapons into our atmosphere."

Sentinel looked at Optimus. He was not used to being contradicted, especially by small organic life forms. "These 'humans' – we call them allies?"

"We have fought as one, Sentinel. I would trust them with my life."

Sentinel gave a small shake of his head, but addressed Mearing politely. "Then I am grateful for your alliance. But hear me and mark my words: The Decepticons must never know the Space Bridge is here. For in their hands, it would mean the end of your world."

On the outskirts of the city, three vague shapes

emerged from the shadows at the side of the road. They were clearly Cybertronian, but unlike most Transformers, these had an almost animalistic form. They were Decepticon Dreads, recently arrived on Earth after stealing a ride on the returning Autobot moon mission. And they were waiting for their master.

A dull rumble turned to a mechanical roar as a huge oil tanker truck rumbled up the road. Its massive shape was silhouetted against the sky as it took on the form of a towering figure.

One of the Dreads addressed the dark shape. "Lord Megatron, your forces are assembled and ready."

"Then upon my command, we strike," came the reply from the darkness.

CHAPTER 10

Sam's apartment, Washington, D.C.

Sam could not get to sleep. He kept thinking about the things Director Mearing had said to him.

"With all due respect, young man, you're not a soldier," she had said. "You're a messenger. You've always been a messenger. And once more, your government thanks you… for delivering the mail."

And then he had been dismissed. Like a little kid, he had been sent home. At least Bumblebee was with him. But that was small comfort to Sam, who felt he deserved a spot on the front lines after all he had been through. After all he had done.

Sam sat up. He might not be working with NEST, but that did not mean he couldn't be involved. He ran out onto his balcony, where Wheelie and Brains sat counting stars. Sam looked below to where

Bumblebee was parked, and called to him.

"Bee, if they're after me again, I want answers. And I say we call in the expert."

Agent Simmons's home, northern Virginia

Former agent Seymour Simmons stormed out of the room. "Interview's over! Outta my house!"

He had been in the middle of a television interview when the questions had begun to take a turn he did not like. He had listened to this pompous news anchor – if what they aired on this network could be called news – for long enough.

"Dutch! DUTCH! Where is my assistant?" Simmons demanded.

Dutch came charging into the room, holding a clipboard in one hand. "Yes, Mr Simmons. Right away, Mr Simmons."

Simmons glared at him. "What's up next? Whadda we got?"

"Book signing at noon, then we pitch your reality show to the producers, followed by dinner," droned Dutch. "Also, this irritating Sam Witwicky keeps calling. He's phoned five times, right now I've got him on hold—"

"The kid? What's he want?" demanded Simmons.

Simmons yanked the headset out of Dutch's ear, and held it to his own. "Sam! How are you? Hey, didn't I tell ya? Shoulda cashed in like me!"

"Simmons," Sam interrupted, "The Decepticons are back. I want to know why. I need your help."

"They're back? Well, that's good for business," replied Simmons.

Sam continued, "What if I told you I know a government secret that you don't?"

Simmons put his hand to his forehead. He looked as if he had suddenly developed a severe headache. He had once worked for the super top secret U.S. government agency called Sector Seven, and he had once known everything there was to know about alien robots. "What kind of government secret?"

"A fifty-year-old alien secret… that nobody ever told you," teased Sam.

"Dutch! Clear my schedule. Get the car. We roll in five."

A few hours later, the door to Sam's apartment burst open. Seymour Simmons, former government agent, pulled off his sunglasses.

"Tell Megatron it's time to tango."

A social club on the boardwalk, Atlantic City, New Jersey

They had all the information they were going to get from the U.S. Space Programme, so Simmons had decided to see what they could learn from Russian history. The Soviet Space Programme had sent numerous unmanned missions to the moon.

Simmons had made a few calls and pulled in some favours. He had a tip that some ex-cosmonauts were living in the United States. Simmons decided to go right to the source, and they were now parked in front of the social club where the cosmonauts were known to meet.

The unlikely band approached a door in the back of the social club. Simmons knocked, and an eye slot slid back to reveal bored, if dangerous-looking, eyes.

Undaunted, Simmons spoke directly into the eye slot: "*Dasvidaniya…* gentlemen."

"*Dasvidaniya* means goodbye," the man answered from behind the door. But he opened it and let Simmons, Sam, and Dutch walk in to the quiet, dimly lit room.

Sam looked around. Three old men played backgammon, while two ladies sat at a table against the far wall.

"Cover the standard-issue henchmen, Agent Witwicky," barked Simmons. "Dutch, gimme something tough to say in Russian."

"My friend, we speak English," offered one of the old men helpfully. "My name is Dmitri. How can we be of service?"

"*Da?* Do you?" mocked Simmons. "Or do you want us to think you do? Line, Dutch, line!"

"Uh . . . *Kalashnikov! Baryshnikov!*" came Dutch's lame reply.

"Dutch, you are useless," Simmons sighed. Turning to the old men, Simmons continued, "Agent Seymour Simmons, Sector… Eight. We know who you are, *cosmonautchiks*. You were supposed to travel to the dark side of the moon. Then it all got shut down. The question is, why?"

"We have seen men like you before," said the old man. "Come to try to buy our silence. We did not fear you then, we do not fear you now. So you tell evil aliens you work for—"

"Evil? We don't work for evil aliens," insisted Sam. "We're with the good ones. All we want to know is what's on the dark side of the moon!"

Dmitri shook his head sadly, but he turned and walked to the corner of the room, where he stopped before a dusty safe that looked as though it had not been touched in years. Dmitri spun the dials, and the door swung open with a rusty whine.

When he came back to the table, Dmitri was carrying a stack of grainy black-and-white photographs. "America first send man to the moon," Dmitri explained. "But USSR first to send cameras. In 1959, we take pictures of dark side, see nothing. But in 1963, we see… this."

Sam looked down at the old photographs.

"Strange rocks," Dmitri continued, pointing to the images. "Hundreds of them."

Sam looked up at Simmons. "I've seen those. They're the pillars for a Space Bridge. Our side found five…"

"Decepticons must've raided the ship before Apollo 11 ever got there," said Simmons, completing Sam's thought. "Took the pillars, and then kept them hidden. Which means they're still up there."

"But it doesn't make sense," said Sam. "If they found the ship and have all those pillars, why'd they leave Sentinel? I mean, if only Sentinel can use them—"

The realisation splashed over Sam like ice-cold water. "He's the one thing they still need! And Optimus just woke him up! Let's get out of here! Bumblebee can find Sentinel – we have to keep him safe!"

CHAPTER II

Interstate 66, Virginia

Bumblebee had no difficulty locating Sentinel Prime, and within an hour an Autobot escort sped down the highway, flanking Sentinel to protect him. Their final destination was NEST headquarters, and they were still about twenty miles from safety.

Bumblebee, with Sam in the driver's seat, led the convoy. Immediately behind him was Mirage, in the form of a red sports car, followed by Sentinel Prime and Sideswipe. Simmons and Dutch brought up the rear, keeping less than a car's length between the front bumper of their white luxury car and the tail-lights of Sideswipe's Corvette mode.

Simmons glanced over his shoulder and saw three black SUVs with flashing blue lights approaching. "Hey, we got help!" he shouted into the radio. "Looks like FBI—" But Simmons cut off mid-sentence as one of the SUVs changed into a terrifying Decepticon Dread named Crankcase without decreasing speed.

"Battle stations!" Simmons cried.

Before anyone could react, Crankcase jumped onto Simmons's luxury car. His claws tore into the roof. But the Dread was too focused on the prey inside the car, and did not notice the overhead highway sign until it was too late. He took the full force of impact to his head and fell backwards off the car. In the process, the luxury car became a convertible.

Dutch gripped the wheel and looked into the rearview mirror. He saw the wreckage of the Dread and the roof but, to his horror, he also saw Simmons tumbling along the road.

Dutch slammed on the brakes, threw the car into reverse, and backed up to where Simmons was slowly picking himself up off the ground. He was bruised and shaken, but otherwise appeared unharmed.

Sam had seen the attack, and now watched as the other two Dreads closed in on the convoy.

"Tell Sentinel to get outta here!" Sam yelled. "You guys cover him. Watch out!"

Sentinel accelerated hard, racing ahead of his protectors and away from the scene of battle.

Sam heard Mirage's voice come over Bumblebee's radio: "Autobots, switch to Stealth Force. Let's take the fight to them!"

Sam watched in awe as Sideswipe, Mirage and Bumblebee partially altered shape. They retained vehicle form, but with bonnets raised, wheelbases extended, and side panels opened, revealing an array of dangerous weapons.

With a squeal of tyres and a smell of burning rubber, all three Autobots executed perfect 180 degree turns and opened fire on the approaching Decepticons.

The Dreads, named Hatchet and Crowbar, realised that they had lost the advantage of surprise. They turned to flee the scene, but Mirage and Sideswipe completed their conversion to robot form and skated after the enemy.

Mirage fired a blast from his arm cannon, sending one of the Decepticons spinning out of control. Leaving it behind, the two Autobots continued their pursuit of the third.

But the damaged Crowbar was not out of the fight. He saw Bumblebee approaching and, in a squeal of burning tyres, drove back onto the road and directly into the path of the oncoming Camaro.

Sam noticed the approaching Decepticon with rapidly growing alarm. "Ah, Bumblebee?"

But Bumblebee was already locked on his target. Accelerating to over 150 miles per hour, Bumblebee showed no sign of dodging out of the path of the oncoming Dread. At the last possible moment, as Sam gripped the wheel and braced himself against the seat, Bumblebee unleashed a barrage from his cannons.

Crowbar was done for and Bumblebee barely slowed down as he zoomed past. "I love this car," Sam said with a smile.

Farther down the road, Mirage and Sideswipe

were closing in on the one remaining target. With Bumblebee now joining the pursuit, Hatchet knew the odds were not in his favour. In an act of desperation, he changed to robot mode, spinning in the air and firing his missiles. Mirage and Sideswipe anticipated the move and easily sidestepped the incoming rockets.

But Bumblebee had a human passenger, and his options were more limited. The missiles locked on to him.

Before he knew what was happening, Sam was flying high through the air. Although he was travelling forward at more than seventy miles per hour, it felt as though he were moving in slow motion. Below him, Bumblebee had changed into robot mode, and with an acrobatic flip worthy of the circus, he dodged the incoming missiles.

Without missing a beat, Bumblebee reached out and grabbed the airborne Sam, and then tucked him back into the driver's seat as he altered modes back into the Camaro.

Sam checked to make sure he was still in one

piece, then groaned, "Please don't ever do that again."

NEST headquarters was in a state of high alert. Lennox had received the message from Sam and was quickly preparing for their unexpected guests – particularly the uninvited ones.

"We've got Decepticons converging on Washington. Optimus is at Andrews Air Force Base… Get him back here now! We need to guard Sentinel. Move every NEST team out and spread through Washington. Make a perimeter."

Ironhide and Ratchet sped out of the hangar and joined Lennox at the main gate. To their relief, the first vehicle they saw was Sentinel Prime's fire engine. Opening the gates, they allowed the former Autobot leader to enter the compound.

Peering down the road, they could see the convoy approaching. Bumblebee still held the lead position, followed closely by Mirage and Sideswipe.

They flew through the gates and screeched to a halt, converting into their robot forms. Sam jumped out of Bumblebee and ran over to Lennox. Looking around, Sam breathed a sigh of relief. Surrounded by seven Autobots and at least fifty highly trained NEST soldiers, he felt confident that they could keep Sentinel safe from Decepticon attack.

"Ironhide!" Lennox shouted. "You three protect Sentinel! The rest of you, guard the perimeter. Watch the road, and the air. Energon sensors will give us only two minutes' warning before the attack."

"Keep him guarded!" Sam repeated. "He's the key!"

Sentinel looked at Sam. "Yes. As I always have been."

Without warning, Sentinel Prime raised his blaster and sent a pulse of plasma tearing through Ironhide. "I am sorry, my Autobot brothers. But we were never going to win the war. For the sake of our planet's survival, a deal with Megatron had to be made."

Ironhide fell to his knees, gravely injured.

"He's with the Decepticons!" Lennox shouted.

Sam had not yet recovered from the shock when

he saw Sentinel level his weapon again, this time at Bumblebee. In the open, with no time to react, Bumblebee was an easy target.

"No… NO! Bumblebee, watch out!" screamed Sam. Bumblebee dodged just in time.

"Get all NEST forces back to base – we're under attack!" Lennox yelled into his radio. "Sentinel Prime is a traitor!"

Sentinel moved off towards the hangar. His shield blocked the blasts from the Autobots' weapons, and he did not even seem to notice the sharp ping of bullets from the NEST soldiers. He headed towards the vault where the five pillars had been placed.

Director Mearing stood between Sentinel and the vault. She surveyed the damage he had done, looking over the smoking ruin of helicopters and NEST vehicles. Disoriented, she looked up. "Sentinel, stop! What are you doing?"

"I am a Prime from the great planet Cybertron. I do not take orders from you. Now return what belongs to me," he demanded. Without waiting for her to respond, Sentinel strode past Mearing and tore the doors off the vault. He reached inside and removed the five pillars. Without any further notice of the destruction and chaos around him, he changed into his vehicle mode.

Sam and Lennox watched as the red fire engine burst from the hangar. Sentinel sped past them, crashing through the gates and out onto the road.

"Sentinel hit the vault and took the pillars," called Mearing.

Lennox got on the radio: "Alert strike teams across the country now! Get Air Force mobilised. We need to hunt this thing."

CHAPTER 12

The National Mall, Washington, D.C.

As night fell over the city of Washington, D.C., the illuminated Lincoln Memorial created an oasis of light on the darkening Mall. Overhead, helicopters flew back and forth, their searchlights prying into corners and hidden spaces.

Moments after a helicopter passed by, Sentinel Prime emerged from the shadows. He carried the five pillars with him. Choosing a spot by the Reflecting Pool, Sentinel placed one of the pillars upright on the ground. He then placed three others a hundred feet apart, so that together they made the four corners of a square. Clutching the fifth pillar in his hands, he waded into the middle of the Reflecting Pool. Standing in the shallow water, Sentinel stood in the middle of the square he had created.

Megatron watched from the steps of the Lincoln Memorial as Sentinel completed his ritual. He then turned and contemplated the silent figure of Abraham Lincoln sitting in its marble hall.

With a single blast from his cannon, Megatron obliterated the figure of Lincoln and took his place in the giant throne.

Starscream arrived on the scene in a roar of jet engines. He climbed the steps of the memorial and admired the new throne of his leader then bowed before Megatron. But Megatron took little notice of his lieutenant. Looking out over the Washington Mall, he saw the familiar shape of Optimus Prime arrive.

"Optimus never knew," he said, more to himself than to Starscream. "When Sentinel left Cybertron, it was to defect. He was to meet me here on Earth… before fate waylaid us both. We needed Optimus and his Matrix to revive Sentinel. The Autobot is so naïve, so predictable. He has done half our work for us."

The National Mall, Washington, D.C.

Optimus Prime looked over the Reflecting Pool to where Sentinel Prime stood. Although he had heard the transmission, had seen the destruction at NEST and Ironhide's injury, he still could not believe Sentinel Prime was a traitor.

As Optimus approached, Sentinel activated the pillar in his hands. Beams of searing white light emitted from the pillar, each connecting to one of the four pillars surrounding Sentinel. The fifth pillar began to rise, carrying the full weight of Sentinel with it, until both were suspended above the Reflecting Pool. A hum of pure energy filled the air.

Optimus looked up at his former mentor. "Sentinel?" he asked. "Why?"

Sentinel ignored him. When he spoke, it was to the voice-activated control of the anchor pillar in his hands. "Power and initiate."

Beams shot up from all five pillars and converged over Sentinel's head, forming a dome of light.

"Commence transport," Sentinel intoned.

The moon

Meanwhile, 238,000 miles away from Washington, D.C., something stirred on the dark side of the moon. All around the wreckage of the Ark, the debris trembled and shifted. Hundreds of hidden Decepticon warriors emerged from the dust, each holding a pillar identical to those used by Sentinel on Earth.

The pillars on the moon began to glow. With a spark of energy, a web of light connected the pillars together, each beam like a spoke on a wheel. In a brilliant flash, the lunar landscape was empty. The Decepticons had disappeared.

The National Mall, Washington, D.C.

The Decepticons from the moon soon came pouring out of the Space Bridge on the Mall. They scattered, trans-scanning vehicles and then flying, driving, or running in every direction. The police were overwhelmed, and the NEST forces were taken completely off guard. Against this surge, nothing could stand.

Megatron sat on his throne, observing the chaos. "Here we are. Fight us now."

"There are too many Decepticons!" shouted Sam. "They're everywhere!"

"Autobots, retreat!" bellowed Optimus. Sam and Lennox looked at each other in disbelief. The past few years had prepared them for many shocks and surprises, but they'd never expected to hear those words uttered by Optimus Prime.

But Optimus did not follow his own orders. Rather than retreat, he charged at Sentinel. Sentinel was the master warrior, though, and had taught Optimus much of what he knew about combat. Almost effortlessly, Sentinel turned Optimus's attack against him, using his forward momentum to flip him onto his back. Sentinel placed his massive foot on Optimus's neck.

Optimus looked up at Sentinel, still craving an explanation. "Why?" he asked again.

"For Cybertron," Sentinel replied. "For our home. What war destroyed, we still can save. But only if we join with the Decepticons… and I knew you never would. It was the only way."

"This is our home," urged Optimus. "We must defend the humans!"

"So lost you are, Optimus. On Cybertron, we were gods. And here… they call us machines."

Sentinel took aim at his old friend, ready to finish him. But a barrage of small arms and rocket fire hit Sentinel, distracting him from the job at hand. He considered destroying the humans, but he could not risk damaging the pillars – he still needed them to bring something much larger to Earth. He gathered them up in his arms and raced into the night.

CHAPTER 13

Dylan Gould estate, Washington, D.C.

Sam's head was spinning from Sentinel's betrayal, the return of Megatron and the Decepticon invasion. But one thought pushed out all others: Keep Carly safe.

He knew her boss was having a party, so he took a taxi to Dylan's home right away. It dropped Sam off in front of a scrollwork iron gate. He walked down the long driveway towards Dylan's mansion, feeling like he had been transported back in time. The place was incredibly huge and ornate.

The party was winding down, and Sam passed very few guests as he made his way through the halls. Then he heard Carly's laugh.

Dylan noticed him standing in the doorway. "Sam! Welcome! Just the guest I was hoping to see."

"I need to talk to my girlfriend about something important," Sam replied. "That okay with you?" Carly knew the look in Sam's eye, so even though she was surprised, she followed him without question. Dylan followed closely behind them, too.

Sam ignored him. They were back outside, and at that moment Dylan was the least of Sam's problems. He needed to get Carly someplace safe, and then he needed to figure out how to stop the Decepticons.

"I really think I could help you, Sam," Dylan was saying. "I remember a talk Dad once had with me. About making hard choices. 'Course, that was way back when Dad's firm was in charge of budget review for NASA…"

Sam stopped in his tracks. NASA?

Dylan continued, pleased by Sam's reaction. "And the thing he taught me was: when it's not your war, you join the side that's gonna win."

That was when Sam noticed Laserbeak, perched atop the main gate of Dylan's estate. Sam's gaze shifted to Dylan's car, sitting in the drive. That was their escape route. He started to move towards the car.

But just then the luxury car changed into Soundwave! The Decepticon grabbed Carly, lifting her into the air, while Dylan's big, burly bodyguard appeared and pinned Sam to the ground.

"Think you're so special, Sam?" Dylan mocked. "So unique? Really think you were the first man ever asked to join the noble alien cause? You know why we haven't returned to the moon since 1972? Because that's the year these two came to my dad. Told him to do some creative accounting and make it far too expensive to ever go back. He and others shut the programme down to keep what was up on the moon a secret."

Sam couldn't believe what he was hearing. It meant the Autobots weren't the only Transformers working with humans – Decepticons had human allies, too! And they had been working with them for decades!

"I've had my eye on you for years, Sam. See, the one spy I could never provide was someone close to the Autobots."

"He'll never work for you," Carly protested, earning a squeeze from Soundwave. She screamed.

Dylan leaned over to Sam and spoke softly. "He will crush her, do you understand me? In the time that it takes you to blink. So try to show a little more respect when someone offers you a job."

Suddenly, Dylan's watch turned into a spider-like robot, scurried across the ground, ran up Sam's leg, and attached itself to Sam's wrist.

"Track down Optimus Prime," Dylan explained, "Because you are the one human he trusts. And you will ask him this question: how does he intend to fight back? We want their tactics, strategy, everything."

"Sam!" Carly cried. "Don't do what he wants!" Soundwave increased his grip on Carly.

"Put her down!" Sam demanded.

"Soundwave!" Dylan ordered. Reluctantly, Soundwave released his grip on Carly and dropped her to the ground.

"You do your job and she'll be safe. You have

my word," Dylan said to Sam.

Dylan's bodyguard roughly escorted Sam to the gate. As he walked off into the night, he heard Dylan calling to him, "You go find your Autobots now. How they plan to fight back – that's all we wanna know."

Once he was through the gate, Sam began to run. His day had gone from bad to worse to much, much worse.

CHAPTER 14

The White House

At the White House, generals and aides ran through the hallways. Any available space had been converted into a war room, and tense voices could be heard in every corridor and doorway.

A man named General Morshower had taken direct command of combat operations. "Our combat commands are now at DEFCON 1 around the globe. We'll have eyes in the sky over the twenty largest U.S. cities within the hour. Colonel Lennox?"

Lennox stepped forward and addressed the group. "We estimate two hundred Decepticons now in hiding. Energon detectors have been triggered as far away as South America. Still no sign of those attack ships we saw come through the Space Bridge."

"We have to assume they're preparing to attack," continued General Morshower, "But so far we don't know when, where, how… or why."

At that moment, an aide ran into the room. "General, the UN just received an encrypted audio file. They say it is from the leader of the Autobots."

"Put it on speaker," Morshower ordered. "Let's hear what they have to say."

As the audio recording began, Morshower looked sharply at Lennox. The voice that was speaking was not the voice of Optimus Prime.

"Defenders of Earth, my name is Sentinel Prime – the true leader of the Autobots. For millennia our galaxy was ravaged by a tragic civil war, but now that war is over, and our armies stand as one. We come from a damaged planet that must be rebuilt. What we need are the natural resources your world has in abundance. Precious metals, iron, steel. We shall use my Space Bridge technology to transport an equitable share of such material. And then we will leave your planet in peace.

"However, for such peace to exist, you must turn

over the rebels you have harboured, or we will deem your intent hostile, and through my Space Bridge will come more battalions. And you will know our righteous strength. We want no war with you, only our planet's reconstruction. Long live Cybertron. We await your reply."

Everyone present looked at one another. Sentinel wanted them to hand over the Autobots. Did they have a choice?

CHAPTER 15

Outside Sam's apartment, Washington, D.C.

The sun was just beginning to rise when Sam wearily dragged himself up the steps to his apartment. The walk from Dylan's estate had taken more than three hours, and even if Megatron himself was waiting in his living room, Sam was going to sit down for five minutes.

But before he could unlock his door, a voice called to him from the bottom of the steps.

"Sam Witwicky?" called a man in a black suit. "FBI. You're a hard man to find. Please come with us."

Sam's shoulders drooped, but he walked back down the stairs and into the waiting sedan. Less than twenty minutes later, the car pulled into a small airport and drove right up to a little jet that was waiting on the tarmac. The FBI agent pointed to the open door, and Sam climbed aboard.

Director Mearing was waiting for him. "Glad they found you. Have a seat and buckle up. We'll debrief you in transit."

Not wanting to reveal any secrets to the Watch-bot on his wrist, Sam tried to protest. "Um, I really don't see how I can be any more help," he argued. "You guys seem so busy… We could just do this later." Then he doubled over in pain. "Ow. Muscle spasm. Ow. Stop it!" The Watch-bot was not going to let him get out of this.

"Sam, I owe you an apology," Mearing said earnestly. "You warned us. You realised Sentinel was the key. I underestimated you at every turn."

"No, hey, you're the expert," offered Sam. "I'm just a walking security risk—ow, ow!" Sam was determined to keep important information from the Decepticons. The Watch-bot was just as determined to keep him on task.

"Are you all right?" asked Mearing.

"No. Ow! Yes."

Director Mearing turned on a TV screen and watched a reporter standing on the steps of the U.S. Capitol. "But after the UN's defiant gesture of offering the Autobots asylum, the U.S. Congress was swift to react, moments ago passing legislation exiling the Autobots from American shores. Our military alliance is over."

"What?" Sam shouted.

Mearing turned to her aide. "It's official. We're going. Tell NEST to begin transport operations."

She turned to Sam. "The reason you are here, Sam, is that if there is anything more you know, anything at all about the enemy's intentions, it's time to tell."

The Watch-bot clamped down on Sam's wrist in a not-so-subtle warning.

"But the Autobots," Sam said. "They can't just leave the planet."

"That's where you're wrong," Mearing replied.

Kennedy Space Center, Cape Canaveral, Florida

Sam looked out the window as the plane banked on its final approach. Below him, Sam could see the Kennedy Space Center. At the launch site, a beat-up looking spacecraft, clearly not entirely of human construction, sat waiting.

Director Mearing explained the scene to Sam. "Its name is the Xantium. It brought the second wave of Autobots five years ago – Sideswipe and the rest. Been under NASA's care and study ever since. With the U.S. government harbouring aliens, we've always wanted an exit option."

"Um, this seems pretty top secret. I should really have clearance," Sam offered in a last effort to keep the information from the Watch-bot.

"Sam, don't worry," said Mearing. "You have clearance with me."

Sam felt anything but reassured.

At the launch site, NASA scientists and engineers were making a final inspection of the spacecraft. After getting off the plane, Sam watched as three hulking Autobots appeared from the far side of the ship.

"The Autobot engineers are known as the Wreckers," explained Mearing. "Roadbuster seems to be the boss, or at least he's always bossing everyone else around. The other two are Topspin and Leadfoot. We never let them off the base because they're not very nice."

As if on cue, Roadbuster began to yell at a NASA scientist. "Gonna be ten thousand pounds of torque on that itsy-bitsy bolt, so it better get twenty and a quarter rotations! Not nineteen. Yer gonna risk the lives of all my friends over one and a quarter screw rotations? Thought we were working with professionals. Oh, what now, ya gonna start crying?"

The NASA scientist looked like he was going to cry, but at that moment, a man came sprinting around the corner and stood toe-to-toe with the Wrecker.

"Back off, you greasy gearhead!" he bellowed. "To your pits!"

He turned to the NASA scientist. "It's okay. Take deep breaths. You just have to focus on his positive intentions."

He turned back to Roadbuster, angry again, and said, "That's a human being you're working with! He's got feelings, doubts and emotions! He's doing the best he can!"

"Tough!" replied Roadbuster. "It's a cold, cruel galaxy! Either the job gets done or it don't."

Sam wasn't as surprised to hear this exchange as he was to see a familiar face. "Epps!" Sam called. "What're you doing here?"

It was Epps's turn to be surprised. "What the… Sam?"

Sam jerked his chin at the Wreckers and raised his eyebrows in a silent question. "Retired from the Air Force," Epps explained. "I just consult, run interference. I kind of know how to talk to them."

Roadbuster was taking advantage of the distraction, and had turned on the scientist again. "Now yer just standing there. Check 'em again! Every weld on those liquid hydrogen lines. Sealed up tight!"

"Hey, hotshot!" yelled Epps. "I said, to your pits!"

The three Wreckers shuffled off to their holding pen, like schoolboys who had just been given a good scolding. Epps followed them and turned on a huge flat-screen television. The Wreckers stood mesmerised by the action of a car race on the TV.

"It's like catnip to them," Epps explained to Sam. He motioned to the ship. "You believe this is really happening?"

Sam looked up at the hulking craft. From up close, it looked barely held together – and yet it was supposed to carry all the Autobots away from Earth. All of Sam's friends. The government was giving Sentinel Prime what he wanted.

"But where's it supposed to take them?" Sam asked.

Epps shook his head sadly. "Any planet but here."

"Clear a path! Outta my way! I want to talk to whoever's in charge!" Seymour Simmons strode across the Tarmac. Sam couldn't have been more surprised.

But Simmons wasn't paying attention to Sam. He only had eyes for the director. "Well, well… Charlotte Mearing."

Director Mearing rolled her eyes. "Former Agent Simmons. I see you managed to survive Washington."

"Washington, Egypt, heartbreak. I survive. It's what I do," replied Simmons. He then turned to Sam.

"They're bringing everybody in, kid. Put all the intel on the table. And what I gotta say is this: If you think deporting the Autobots solves anything—"

"This has gone way above my pay grade, Agent," Mearing answered. "If there's a war for Earth, humans will fight it."

"Well," – Simmons laughed darkly – "It won't be much of a fight. Spent my life studying this alien species. This is what I know. This is who I am. Those Autobots are the only chance we have."

"They might be," said Mearing. "But it's out of

my hands."

Sam watched as the other Autobots arrived and lined up to board the Xantium. He couldn't believe this was actually happening. The last hope for humanity was about to leave for ever.

The Watch-bot prodded Sam, and he remembered Carly. He had to warn Optimus, but he had to do it without the little Decepticon noticing.

"Optimus!" Sam called. Optimus strode over to Sam and crouched down to get close to eye level. Sam saw sadness in his eyes, and something else, too. Disappointment… in himself.

"What your leaders say is true," Optimus said. "All this was my fault. I told them whom to trust. I was wrong."

"That doesn't make it your fault," Sam consoled him. "It just makes you human for a change." Sam couldn't look Optimus in the eye. He couldn't face his old friend knowing that Decepticons were listening, watching, waiting for any bit of information they could use against the Autobots. And against Earth.

Optimus shook his head. "Remember this, Sam: you may lose your faith in us, but never in yourselves." The huge robot turned to leave, but the Watch-bot bit Sam, forcing him to call Optimus back.

Through the pain, Sam called, "Optimus, I need to know how you're gonna fight back!"

Puzzled by Sam's behavior, Optimus turned back to listen.

"You're coming back, right?" Sam asked. "You have some plan? You'll bring help, reinforcements, something? What's the strategy? You can tell me. No other human will ever know."

Optimus was the leader of the Autobots for a reason. He immediately recognised that Sam was trying to tell him there was more here than met the eye.

"You know we'd never be able to live with ourselves," Sam continued, "If we just do what they want."

"You are my friend, Sam. You always will be," Optimus reassured him. "But your leaders have spoken. From here, the fight will be your own." Optimus turned and boarded the Xantium. All the Autobots were now on board, except for one. Bumblebee paused, looking back at Sam.

"Wait, Bumblebee! Bumblebee!" Sam called.

Bumblebee walked back to Sam and, in his broken voice, said, "I… will… never… forget you… Sam."

"This is your home," Sam insisted. "Earth is your home."

Bumblebee gently touched Sam's chest. "I will always… be… here. Fight them… for ever." Bumblebee then turned and boarded the ship. He did not look back again.

Sam watched as the ship began to lift off the platform, huge boosters pushing the rocket skyward. As it left the Earth behind, the Xantium accelerated, a high-pitched whine emanating from within the steady bass roar of the boosters.

The first-stage booster disengaged and dropped away towards Earth, its descent slowed by two huge parachutes. With the ignition of the secondary booster, the Xantium pushed further towards the heavens.

Sam's phone rang. The caller ID read DYLAN GOULD.

"Well?" Sam asked angrily. "You get what you wanted?"

"That Bumblebee is so adorable," Dylan gloated. "But that Optimus… Come on, that guy needs to learn to lighten up!"

"You wanted an answer, you got one," Sam replied. "There was no strategy. They're gone."

"We thank you, Sam. We just needed to be sure."

"Sure of what?" asked Sam.

"That they'd go without a fight. And all wrapped up in a tight, clean package."

Above the distant thunder of the ascending rocket, a new sound, closer and more urgent, began to push its way into Sam's consciousness. It increased from a distant rumble to a thundering roar in seconds.

An F-22 Raptor suddenly raced across the sky in pursuit of the rocket. And it was gaining quickly.

Sam knew in an instant who it was – Starscream!
"NO!" shouted Sam.

Starscream fired his cannons. In a massive
explosion, the Xantium disintegrated into a
fine, sparkling powder. Starscream circled back,
waggling his wings in triumph as he flew over the
stunned audience. At the same time, barely noticed
by Sam, the Watch-bot dropped from his wrist and
scuttled away like an evil spider.

Simmons wheeled up and paused next to Sam.
Then he turned to meet the eyes of a stunned Director
Mearing. "And now you know what happens," he
told her, "When you do what the Decepticons want."

After the initial shock, Sam jumped into action.
He got Epps and Simmons (trailed by his assistant,
Dutch) together and spoke urgently. "I need your
help to track a phone call," he told them. "There's
a guy out there running the whole Decepticons–
human operation. He took my girlfriend hostage."

Simmons turned to his guy. "Dutchie! Let's play.
As in dirty."

Sam was amazed to see Dutch spring into action.

Like a seasoned pro, he commandeered a computer console, hooked Sam's mobile phone into it, and began to rapidly hit the keys. In seconds, Dutch had a hit. "Call was placed en route, Chicago mobile sites, just hacked into the phone's camera. Looks like downtown, someplace high… It's this building in the photo!"

"I'm going," said Sam. "I have to save her."

"You're not going alone," said Epps. "NEST is preparing for war, but let me call Lennox, round up whoever they can spare."

"Why are you helping me?" asked Sam.

Epps stopped and looked at Sam. "Because the Autobots were my friends, too."

Sam and Epps jumped into one of the government SUVs and sped away, while Simmons went after Director Mearing.

"I want in the mix, now," he told her. "I have dedicated my life to beating this Decepticon scum. Not you. Not your yes men. Me."

Mearing, defeated, nodded and let him board her plane, headed for Washington.

CHAPTER 16

Dylan Gould's penthouse apartment, Chicago, Illinois

Dylan and Carly rode the freight lift to the roof of a Chicago skyscraper with the pillars that Sentinel had rescued. Carly was a hostage, but she still might get a chance to contact Sam. If she did, he and NEST would need all the information they could get, so she started asking questions.

"What does it mean, their planet needs our 'resources'?" she asked.

Dylan looked at her and chuckled. "What do you think those really are? Iron, metal, steel? They could mine all that from you-name-it galaxy. Why here? What's here and nowhere else?"

Then it dawned on her. "Us."

Dylan nodded. The freight lift doors opened;

they had reached the roof. Dylan led the way, explaining as they walked. "Can't rebuild without a labour force. How many rocks out there in the universe offer six billion workers?"

"But you can't transport all these people to their planet," Carly insisted. "We wouldn't survive!"

"They're not going to be shipping anything there," Dylan revealed. "They're shipping their planet here." Dylan pushed open the door on the roof, and he and Carly walked out into the bright sunlight. Standing before them were the menacing figures of Sentinel Prime and Megatron.

Dylan continued, "Look at these two. Takes your breath away, doesn't it? Their war destabilised their galaxy ages ago... destroyed their planet and half its stars... the whole thing is doomed. So these two worked out a secret deal."

"To move their whole planet?" asked Carly incredulously.

Dylan nodded. "They're spreading hundreds more pillars across the Earth as we speak. So they can launch them into orbit by morning."

Sentinel ignored the humans and began placing the Space Bridge pillars at the four corners of the building's roof. He then placed the anchor pillar on top of the spire that jutted from the centre of the roof.

"That's the control one," Dylan offered. "It needs to stay anchored by Earth's magnetic core. I think it's magnetic. Or kinetic. It's something. Anyway, tomorrow morning… bang!"

Carly stared at Dylan. "You actually want this to happen."

Dylan smiled. "They'll need human leaders."

"And you want to be CEO," Carly said.

"Don't jinx it for me. We had a good long run, we really did. But we don't own this planet. We've just been renting."

Carly was alone, trapped in Dylan's penthouse apartment across the river from the skyscraper. She walked around the living room in a daze of fear and frustration. She could handle the fear, if she could just be doing something. She looked out across the

Chicago River, towards the building where Sentinel continued work on the Space Bridge. That was when she noticed Dylan's telescope.

Looking through it, she could see Sentinel and Megatron. She couldn't hear what was being said, of course, but the actions of the two Cybertronians were difficult to misinterpret.

They seemed to be arguing. Suddenly, Sentinel lashed out, pinning Megatron to the wall, gripping his throat and getting right in his face.

Carly stepped back from the telescope, pondering what she had just seen. She didn't have to read metallic lips to know that Megatron had just been humiliated. And she got the impression that Sentinel had plans to be in charge, by himself.

CHAPTER 17

City limits, Chicago

Sam, Epps, and a few of Epps's old army buddies drove into Chicago. Even for battle-hardened men the sight was shocking. For Sam, it was simply unbelievable. The Decepticons had destroyed the city. Fires raged everywhere, buildings had been toppled, rubble and wrecked cars were strewn about the streets.

The four stared in stunned silence, until one of the soldiers snapped them out of it. "INCOMING!"

A Decepticon fighter had turned in their direction and, spotting them, closed in. They were completely exposed. No place to hide, no chance to run.

But a sudden laser blast caught the fighter and knocked it out of the sky. Sam looked around for the source of the blast; no human weapon could have done that kind of damage to a Decepticon.

He stared in disbelief as Optimus Prime walked into view from behind a ruined building. Bumblebee, Ratchet and the rest of the Autobots followed him. Sam's mouth dropped open.

Optimus said to Sam, "Perhaps your leaders will now understand: Decepticons will never leave your planet alone. And we needed them to believe we had gone."

"They were watching me!" Sam stammered. "I couldn't tell you…"

"You told me enough to know something was wrong," Optimus reassured him.

Sam still couldn't understand, couldn't quite believe his own senses. "But your ship… They blew it up…"

"Designed the thing, didn't we?" said Roadbuster. "First booster rocket to separate: That was our escape pod! Thing was a bucket of bolts anyway – never would have made it outta the atmosphere."

Optimus looked around them at the ruins of Chicago. "If they're destroying the city, it's to make a fortress. So no one can see what they're up to inside."

"Then I think I know where to look," said Sam, thinking of the building they had found by tracing Dylan's mobile phone. He pointed to the Decepticon fighter that Optimus had shot down. "Can we sneak in with that thing?"

"Get to work, boys," Roadbuster ordered. "I want this enemy ship top-tight ready."

The Wreckers pounced on the ship, and Sam watched as they repaired the damage from Optimus's blast using pieces of vehicles and equipment found in the devastation around them. Sam thought they looked just like a pit crew at a car race.

They were finished in less than an hour. Bumblebee climbed into the cockpit, followed by Sam, who was thrilled to be with his friend again.

"You think it'll fly?" Sam asked.

Bumblebee nodded.

"And you do know how to fly it?" Sam asked.

Bumblebee wobbled his hand, mimicking the human gesture for so-so.

"Whoa, wait, what does that mean? Bee, explain that…" Bumblebee pretended he didn't hear, and pushed the throttle. Sam was thrown back into the co-pilot seat, where he looked in vain for a seat belt.

Back on the ground, Epps gave a command: "Let's move out!" The force headed to Dylan's building by air and by ground.

Bumblebee piloted the captured fighter alongside the skyscraper. Gradually, so as not to attract too much attention, he rose up the side of the building until he was level with an apartment balcony. The ship stopped one floor below the apartment where Carly now paced.

The hatch opened and Sam climbed out onto the front of the ship. It was a jump of only about three feet from the ship to the balcony, but he was also sixty storeys off the ground. It took Sam a few moments and a deep breath before he made the leap.

After landing safely on the balcony, Sam quietly opened the sliding door and sneaked inside. He found a staircase and took it up to the top level of the penthouse. From the living room, he could hear

Dylan and Carly's voices.

Sam moved with grim determination, slowly and quietly. He was so focused on surprising Dylan that he did not notice when the stereo system he had just snuck past silently turned into Laserbeak!

Dylan's attention was focused out the window, and Sam saw his chance.

"Shh… Carly!" he whispered. But just as Carly turned in surprise, Laserbeak attacked. The vulture-like Decepticon threw Sam over the couch and pinned him to the carpet.

"Sam!" Carly shouted.

Dylan turned to the scene in his living room with shock. "Laserbeak!"

Laserbeak raised his arm cannon and blew out one of the panoramic windows. He dragged Sam to the edge and pushed him over the side. Sam disappeared from sight.

"No!" Carly screamed, lunging after him, but Dylan grabbed her and held her back.

Laserbeak turned away from the window, satisfied with his work. He did not see the

Decepticon attack ship that rose into view behind him, with Sam crouched on top.

From inside the ship, Bumblebee opened fire, blasting Laserbeak against the wall. Dylan threw himself on the ground, cowering behind the couch.

Carly immediately ran to the edge. Sam stood ready, his hand extended. She leapt, and he pulled her aboard.

Sam got Carly into the cockpit with Bumblebee and was about to climb in himself when he was yanked back by Laserbeak. As the Decepticon aimed his blaster, an unmanned U.S. Air Force drone zipped through and took the blast but knocked Sam and Laserbeak backwards onto the deck of the ship. The drone spun out of control, crashing into the ship's stabilisers.

Bumblebee could barely control the rocking ship; it began a slow, spiralling descent. Laserbeak, enraged at missing, aimed his blaster again just as Sam yelled, "Bumblebee, FIRE!"

Realising too late that Sam had manoeuvred him right in front of the ship's cannons, Laserbeak couldn't dodge the missile fire. He fell to the street below.

The same street that, Sam now noticed, was approaching very quickly. Sam braced himself, and the ship landed hard.

Carly, shaken, got out of the cockpit, and walked, trembling, to Sam. She placed her hands on his face: "You… found me…" Sam and Carly hugged, sharing a brief moment of peace in the surrounding chaos.

The moment did not last long. Having watched much of the action from the street below, Epps and his team, along with the Autobots, rushed to the crash site.

Epps noticed the damaged drone resting on the ground. He grabbed it and began speaking directly into the drone's surveillance array.

"Flight control copy? Rotate, do something!" The drone was supposed to send satellite feeds back to the Air Force with information. Epps was hoping to send a message.

The drone was motionless. But just as Epps was

about to give up in disgust, the drone's optic sensor began to move. It focused on Epps and nodded up and down several times.

Sam ran over to join Epps. Looking into the drone's eye, he began to shout instructions. "If you can hear us, Sentinel is here in Chicago, getting ready to launch the pillars."

CHAPTER 18

NEST headquarters, outside Washington, D.C.

Outside of Chicago, the U.S. government and all its agencies were frantically scrambling to put a plan together. The small drone had sent back video showing nothing but destruction. Other than that, it had become a total blackout, with no information coming out of the destroyed city. They had no idea what was happening, or how to help.

Back at NEST headquarters, Simmons, Director Mearing, and General Morshower tried to come up with defence plans. Simmons had one idea. He got Colonel Lennox on the phone. "Lennox, listen up. You have the only guys close enough who know anything about how to fight these things."

The general agreed, adding, "Sending full combat teams now won't work. There are too many of them. But a stealth strike from your team might work."

"I can't tell you what to do, soldier," Simmons continued, "but if I wasn't stuck here, I think you know where I'd be."

Just after they signed off, a feed started to come in from the drone. Simmons and Mearing struggled to make sense of the garbled communications. The visual images kept scrambling, and the audio was breaking up. They concentrated on the grainy image, where they kept catching glimpses of Sam's face to go with the broken audio.

"Sentinel's pillars… atop building… skyscraper… to open another Space Bridge!"

Simmons looked up at the general. "Get Colonel Lennox back on the line. Now!"

Grissom Airbase, twelve miles north of Kokomo, Indiana

Lennox sat at a desk, frustrated and uncertain. When an image of Sam suddenly appeared on the screen, Lennox jumped out of his seat.

He could just make out Sam's words as they

came through the speakers.

"...will... transport... Cybertron here... have to... destroy... control pillar! Shoot it down!"

Lennox signalled to two of the soldiers on his team. Not wanting to miss a word Sam was saying, he wrote his orders on paper: "Get me technical readouts of the tallest building in Chicago."

The feed from Sam in Chicago was suddenly cut off, but it was quickly replaced by the voice of Simmons. "You hearing him, Lennox? If you're going, the time is now!"

Lennox didn't need prodding. He had already grabbed his gear and called for a full assembly of his team.

CHAPTER 19

Chicago

Dylan Gould was not happy. He had lost his hostage, Sam had survived, Laserbeak was destroyed and, worst of all, his apartment was completely ruined.

The only thing that kept him going was the knowledge that the Decepticons would rule, and Dylan would have a place of power among them. He was valuable, and he was about to prove it once again.

Sentinel and Megatron still did not know that Optimus and the Autobots were alive and in Chicago. Dylan was going to deliver that warning. He ran through the streets and towards the bridge that spanned the Chicago River, waving a white T-shirt over his head. It was important that the Decepticons did not mistake him for an enemy, so he kept calling, "The Autobots are alive! They are here!"

Looking down from his perch far above the city, Sentinel Prime took notice of Dylan and tuned his auditory sensors to pick up the sound of his voice.

Hearing the message, Sentinel turned to Megatron. "Remind me again, what exactly is your army good for?" he asked icily.

Megatron stood stunned, but only for a moment. "Decepticons," he roared, "Guard the pillars. Destroy the Autobots!"

Far below on the street, the bridge began to open, its two halves reaching towards the sky. Dylan barely made it across, leaping over the gap and tumbling down the other side.

Sentinel looked at his control panel. "The magnetic polarity is achieved. Activate assembly."

At his command, all around the world pillars rose high into the stratosphere. Once in position, each pillar emitted a beam of light, joining it with the next pillar. In moments, a ring of searing light encircled the globe.

Sentinel looked up at the arc of light that split the sky above Chicago and uttered a single word: "Initiate."

A jagged bolt of energy shot skyward from the anchor pillar.

On the ground, Sam saw what was happening. "It's starting!" he called. Sam hoped that his message had gotten through. He looked off in the distance, towards the tall building where Sentinel had set up his pillars. "Can we shoot the anchor pillar down? It controls everything." he asked Epps.

Epps looked at it sceptically, shaking his head. "Eight blocks away – gotta get closer for the shot, and it's across the river. Gonna have a hell of a time sneaking up." They set out for the bridge.

Meanwhile, a very small group of reinforcements had arrived. Flying so low their rotors turned the surface of Lake Michigan into white foam, five tiltrotor aircraft closed in on Chicago. Inside the lead Osprey, Lennox and his team wore specially modified wing suits. He was confident his team knew the drill by heart, but he turned to them for one last briefing.

"When the Osprey gets enough altitude, we jump. Aim your descents towards the river. Follow tight. Get to the bridge."

Lennox and his men jumped, and they soared through the city like giant flying squirrels. The wing suits caught the airflow and created a drag that both slowed the soldiers' descent and allowed them a remarkable degree of manoeuvrability. And they needed it: within moments, a Decepticon fighter had targeted them and was closing in on their position.

Making a hard bank to the left, Lennox led his team through a narrow gap in a crumbling building. The attack ship tried to follow, but was destroyed in a spectacular explosion when its wing caught the edge of the building.

All eight soldiers deployed their parachutes and landed safely on the roof of a parking garage. Moments later they were out of their jump gear and had regrouped in a sheltered corner of the garage.

Lennox's team found Sam, Carly and Epps underneath the bridge. Lennox was happy to see his old army buddy Epps, despite the danger. "So this is retired, huh?" he whispered.

"Don't start with me," Epps answered. "I'm armed and I'm angry. We can't get across to the building. And the Autobots are surrounded up there." The humans could hear the booms of the Autobots fighting off Shockwave and the Driller. The Autobots had taken fire for them when Shockwave attacked, and the men needed to move quickly to take advantage of the diversion.

Lennox received a transmission from NEST headquarters. "Here's the good news," he told his friend. "Thanks to our friend Simmons, missiles are inbound in twenty minutes. Have your men in position to laze targets."

Epps nodded. Lennox looked around them. "But we need to find a route across the river." As if on command, the bridge began to lower.

Sam smiled. He had a feeling their friend Simmons and his assistant, Dutch, had come through once again.

Optimus Prime had pulled his flight harness from his mobile battle kit and now soared overhead, opening fire on the metallic Driller beast, destroying tentacles and punching huge holes in its sides. Its remaining tentacles writhing like wounded snakes, the Driller lay otherwise still in a ruinous heap.

Shockwave felt no emotion at the loss. He certainly was not sad that his pet had been killed. But he was irritated that his long hours of research and work had come to this end. Sighting his massive cannon on Optimus Prime, he unleashed a barrage of fire.

The blasts caught Optimus's harness, destroying the propulsion system. Spiralling out of control, Optimus crashed into the side of a building and became entangled in debris.

Meanwhile, Bumblebee had engaged Soundwave in a fierce battle. But he was quickly outnumbered as more Decepticons arrived to flank him. Bumblebee was Soundwave's prisoner.

But two of the smallest Transformers set out to be two of the biggest heroes. Wheelie and Brains had arrived in Chicago with the other Autobots, but not really being the fighting type, they had remained hidden during the battle. Even so, they had kept close enough to the action to observe what was happening, and when they saw Bumblebee being taken down, they decided it was time to get involved.

They couldn't take on Soundwave and his Decepticon warriors on their own, but Wheelie had a plan.

In all the commotion, none of the Decepticons noticed two small service 'bots as they made their way through the rubble, up the side of a building, and onto the hull of a huge Decepticon battle cruiser that was suspended over the Autobot prisoner.

The cruiser hovered above Soundwave, with Wheelie and Brains sitting in the abandoned pilot seat. Wheelie scanned the control panel. "'Do not use in flight,'" he read aloud.

"Better not push that," Brains offered. "We're in flight."

"Exactly the point." Wheelie pushed the button.

At that particular moment, Soundwave was enjoying his moment of triumph over Bumblebee. But it was short-lived. Suddenly, the attack ships nested in the Battle Cruiser's hull began to fall to the ground. Wheelie had pressed the release button! Many of the ships fell right on top of Decepticon warriors.

Using the chaos as cover, Bumblebee rose to his feet and aimed his cannon. Soundwave would never trouble the Autobots again.

But Bumblebee wasn't out of danger. While he had been fighting, the evil Shockwave had come up from behind him. Bumblebee had nowhere to run, and stood facing the menacing one-eyed Decepticon.

Just then a shadow passed overhead. Finally free of debris, Optimus slammed into Shockwave with such force that the Decepticon was thrown backwards on the ground.

Optimus did not let up. He was on Shockwave in an instant, pounding him with his huge fists. Shockwave struggled, but could not free himself from Optimus's iron grip.

The Autobots quickly defeated their foe, and Optimus moved on to his next opponent: Sentinel Prime.

CHAPTER 20

Chicago

Overhead, the connection between the anchor pillar and those in the sky was complete. A web of light stretched across the sky. Sentinel looked up, satisfied with his work.

"It's our world now," he said. "Commence transport."

Optimus arrived on the street below and looked up at Sentinel defiantly, raising his cannon. Sentinel moved to dodge the blast, realising too late that he was not the target. Optimus fired, blowing apart the spire upon which the anchor pillar rested.

With a cry, Sentinel reached for the anchor pillar, but he was too late and it tumbled to the street below.

Optimus gazed up at the robot who was once

his friend. "You are defeated, Sentinel Prime. Your allies are destroyed; your plans will fail. Come down and face me, and let us be done with this."

"This game is not done, Optimus, not while I live. You are still outnumbered... Decepticons! Trigger the pillar!"

Sentinel Prime leapt down from the roof, crashing to the ground to confront his former student.

Optimus and Sentinel circled each other warily, looking for weakness, for a chance to strike.

"You were the one who taught me freedom is the right of all sentient beings," said Optimus.

"Yes," replied Sentinel, "But survival is the right of the fittest."

Sam had watched the anchor pillar fall from the roof. At first he expected the Space Bridge to close automatically, but nothing happened. Even from the ground, the anchor pillar continued to power the energy grid.

When Sam heard Sentinel's command to the Decepticons, he knew he had to do something.

Turning to Carly, he said, "Stay here. I have to do this."

He ran through the streets towards the fallen pillar. But he saw another figure approaching the same spot.

It was Dylan, and he reached the pillar first.

"Stop, Dylan," Sam pleaded. "Please don't!"

Dylan looked at Sam and smiled. "There's only one future for me." He pushed the ancient Transformer symbol etched on the pillar.

The city seemed to buckle as a sonic boom washed over it. The energy grid in the sky above blazed with a brilliant intensity, then went black. And then Sam saw it – the curvature of an immense metal planet, pushing itself into the atmosphere.

For a moment Dylan was too busy watching Cybertron emerge through the Space Bridge to notice Sam rushing him. Even so, he managed to push Sam away and pick up a metal pipe from the pile of building rubble. Sam stood back, eyeing Dylan's weapon warily.

Behind Dylan, the anchor pillar continued to

blast its stream of pure plasma energy into the sky, drawing Cybertron ever nearer. Sam could actually feel the thrum of electricity emanating from the beam.

"You chose sides. You chose wrong," mocked Dylan. "You see that planet up there? I just rescued a whole other world. You think you're a hero?"

"No," said Sam. "Just a messenger."

And with that, Sam knocked the pillar out of Dylan's hands. But it was too late.

Cybertron had come to Earth.

Seeing Sam and Optimus struggle with their own opponents, Carly set out alone, on a mission of her own. It was time for her to take action, and she knew exactly who was going to help her.

She finally found him, sitting in an alley, looking up at the sky: Megatron.

Carly climbed up onto the wreckage of a city bus so that she could stand face-to-face with the leader of the Decepticons.

"So, Megatron," she began. "May I ask you a

question? Was it worth it?" Carly leaned in closer. "All your work, to bring Sentinel back? When clearly he now has all the power. I just find it ironic. Almost tragic, really. Your Decepticons finally conquer this planet, and yet their leader won't be you."

Megatron was seething. He could crush this insect in an instant. But he was listening, because what the human was saying was no more nor less than the sum of his own thoughts.

"Any minute now," Carly continued relentlessly, "You'll be nothing but Sentinel's servant."

Pride got the best of him. Megatron stood, the red of his eyes blazing brightly again. He looked over to where Optimus and Sentinel fought. "How ironic indeed," he said, "To watch my two greatest enemies battling each other."

Then he made his decision.

Sentinel slammed Optimus to the ground. His old student had put up a good fight, but it was time to end this. He could sense that Optimus had little fight left in him. Sentinel recovered his rust cannon and took aim at Optimus.

"Always the bravest of us," said Sentinel. "But you could never make the hard decisions, Optimus. Our planet will survive. Thanks to us. Farewell, old friend."

But before he could pull the trigger, Sentinel felt his arm being wrenched from behind. The blaster was knocked out of his grip. Sentinel turned to find the source of this outrage, and looked into the eyes of his former conspirator.

"Megatron!" Sentinel exclaimed.

"Lord Megatron, to you."

Megatron hit Sentinel with a punch that lifted him off the ground and sent him sprawling in the dust. Sentinel recovered quickly, but when he rose to his feet, he saw Megatron and Optimus standing side by side.

Sentinel chuckled. "We were gods once, all of us. But here, there will be only one."

The battle that ensued shook the very foundations of the city. Even with their forces combined, Megatron and Optimus found Sentinel a fierce opponent. The three beat upon one another mercilessly.

The turning point came when Megatron landed a mighty kick, sweeping Sentinel's legs out from under him. Sentinel was up again in an instant, but the move had bought Optimus the time he needed. He stood facing Sentinel, the cosmic rust blaster in his hand.

Sentinel took the blast in the chest. He looked down, stunned, and watched as the corrosive element began to spread over his frame. Sentinel fell to his knees before Optimus.

Lennox and Epps had not been idle. While the three Transformers had been locked in an epic battle, the humans had been planting explosives on and around the anchor pillar. After lighting the short fuse, the two soldiers sprinted for cover behind a pile of rubble.

The explosion destroyed the pillar. In the sky, the energy grid of the Space Bridge flickered and went out. The massive form of Cybertron faded, and then disappeared completely.

Megatron's wail of despair could be heard for miles when he saw Cybertron vanish. He knew that his plans had failed. At long last, Optimus Prime was the ultimate victor.

Defeated, Megatron turned to Optimus for mercy. "Please, a truce is all I want. Remember, brother, we once held the same values, the same dreams. Freedom for all Transformers, life for our home world, for Cybertron. Our means may have diverged, but our ends were never so far apart. All I ask for is peace, a chance to rebuild our planet, a chance to return home."

"There is no peace through tyranny, Megatron," Optimus replied. "I wonder if you will ever learn that. You will have your truce, but be gone from this place. Leave this planet so that its people, at least, may have peace."

Optimus turned his attention back to the dying Sentinel Prime. Sentinel reached up with a trembling hand, which Optimus ignored.

"All I ever wanted," Sentinel gasped, "was survival. You must see… why I had to betray you…"

"You didn't betray me. You betrayed yourself," said Optimus, turning away.

The battle was done.

EPILOGUE

Sam joined the group surrounding Optimus Prime. He had helped save the world, again. But this time he had more help. He felt a hand slip into his and looked up to see Carly standing beside him.

"I love you, Carly," Sam said. "I promise I'll make this all up to you."

"You promise?"

"Promise," Sam insisted.

"And just how are you going to make it up to me?" Carly teased.

Suddenly Bumblebee coughed and spluttered. Sam looked on with concern. "You choking on something, Bee? Can you even choke on something?" Sam asked.

But Bumblebee coughed out a small gasket ring and handed it to Sam.

"Okay, hold on, hang on," Sam said as he realised what was going on. "Bumblebee! I'm not ready to propose!"

Carly just smiled and patted Bumblebee. "I love this car," she said.

In any war, there are calms between storms. There will be days when we lose faith. Days when our allies turn against us... but the day will never come that we forsake this planet and its people.

For I am Optimus Prime... and I send this message to the universe: We are here. We are home.